Cheeky Charlie!

Written and illustrated by

Ben Redlich

little bee

FOR
MY BROTHER,
CHARLIE.
B.R.

First published in 2007
by Meadowside Children's Books
185 Fleet Street, London EC4A 2HS
This edition published in 2008 by
Little Bee, an imprint of Meadowside Children's Books

Text and Illustrations © Ben Redlich
The right of Ben Redlich to be identified
as the author and illustrator has been asserted
by him in accordance with the Copyright,
Designs and Patents Act, 1988

A CIP catalogue record for this book
is available from the British Library

10 9 8 7 6 5 4 3 2 1
Printed in Malaysia

One lowly day,
Charlie the monkey was bored.

"So much time, so little to do."
Charlie yawned,
"I need a good laugh!"

So pretty soon, Charlie decided
to wander out and find some entertainment.

Before long he saw Ostrich and Tortoise.

Charlie pranced
around in front
of Ostrich pretending to fly.

"You flying south
this winter?" he said,
knowing full well she
couldn't fly.

"I'm sorry," said Charlie, sniggering under his breath.
"I didn't hear you.
Can you say that again a little slower!?"

"Don't be cheeky, Charlie!" said Tortoise,
so Charlie pushed on in search of more amusement.

After a while he saw Zebra grazing.
Charlie started laughing at him.

"Hey, horse-face!" he jeered, "nice pyjamas!"

"Oh! Don't be cheeky, Charlie!"
said Zebra.

"Be on your way!"

Pretty soon Charlie spotted
Leopard lazing.
Charlie pointed and mocked.

"Hey spotty," he heckled.
"That's the worst case of
          measles I've ever seen!"

"Don't be cheeky, Charlie," sighed Leopard.
      "I wouldn't change my spots even if I could!"

But just then Charlie spied Mandrill
and almost fell over giggling.

"Nice face paint!" he screamed.
"Which circus do you belong to?!"

"Don't be cheeky, Charlie!" snarled Mandrill.

"I don't think I'm the biggest clown around here!"

But Charlie carried on.
   Soon he was completely giddy and out of control.
                  He mocked Warthog...

...teased Giraffe...

...and howled
at Elephant.

Great and small,
Charlie was cheeky to everyone he met.

Then, Charlie saw one of the
funniest things he'd ever seen.

It was his brother Furley.

"Hey rosey-cheeks!" he sniggered.
"Does it hurt to sit?!"

Furley felt confused, as Charlie laughed himself stupid.

"Don't be cheeky, Charlie!"
Furley warned.
"Take a look around you!"

But Charlie the monkey couldn't speak...
the more he looked, the more he laughed.

"I think," said Furley,
"you had better take a look at yourself..."

Charlie looked over his shoulder and squealed,

"AHHHHRRRGH"

His brother and his friends weren't the only ones with bright pink bottoms!

Very quickly, cheeky Charlie stopped his cheeky insults...

...scampered away...

and hid for the rest of the day.